The Red Lemon

by Bob Staake

Dragonfly Books ⟶ New York

Over the hills
and along the blue sea,

"The lemons are ready!" shouts Farmer McPhee.

"They soaked up the sun,
and drank all the rain.
We'll pick 'em and ship 'em
to stores via train!

"There's nothing like lemons.
This fruit isn't mellow.

They're tangy!
They're tasty!
They're tart—
and soooooo
yellow!"

Bright yellow lemons for miles and miles!
Bright yellow lemons give farmers big smiles!

Lemons
for sherbet and
lemons for pie!

Lemons
for drinks on
the Fourth of July!

Lemons
for cookies and
sweet birthday cakes!

Lemons
for muffins and
fresh fruity shakes!

crunchy lemon 'n' ginger snaps

fresh-squeezed lemonade

lemon chiffon cream cake

lemon pie

lemon nut muffin

sherbet

citrus shake

SNIFF 'em, and **PICK** 'em, and **PACK** 'em in a crate.

Bright yellow lemons, so tasty, so great!

"Wait just a minute!
That one overhead!
That lemon's not yellow.
My goodness, it's *red!*

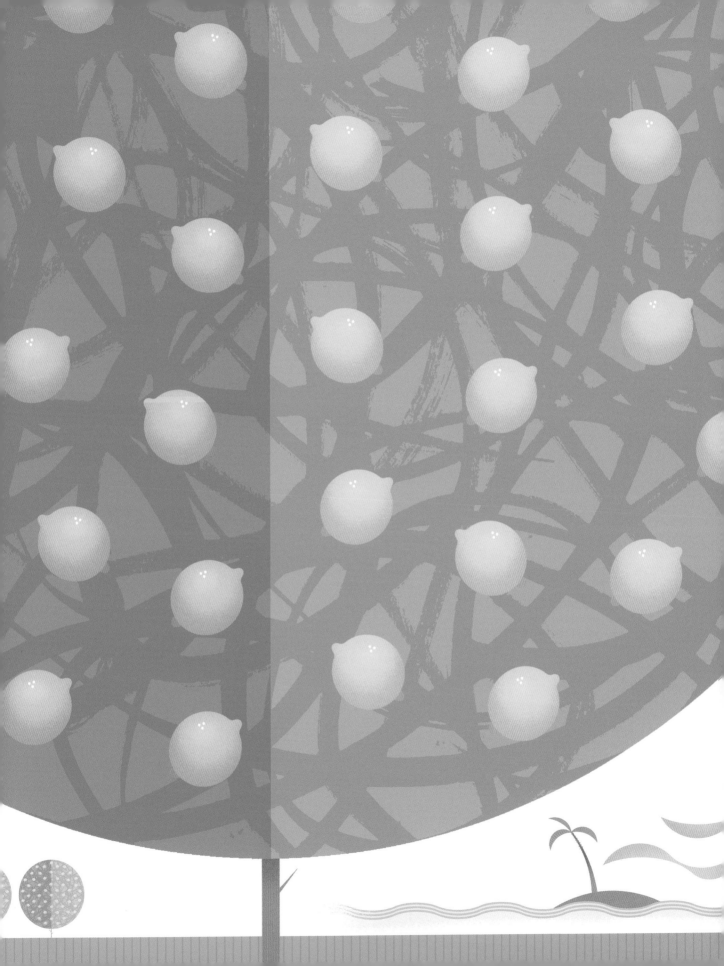

"It's as red as a stop sign!
It's as red as a rose!
I can't have red lemons
where yellow fruit grows!
Imagine a world where
lemonade's red!
Where once-yellow cupcakes
are crimson instead!

"When people bite into a
fruit that they chew,
they count on it being
the *right*-colored hue!
Who'd squeeze this *red* thing
in their afternoon tea?
Who'd buy a *red* lemon
from Farmer McPhee?

"This lemon
must go!
It's too red
to bear!
And so this
red lemon
I'll . . .

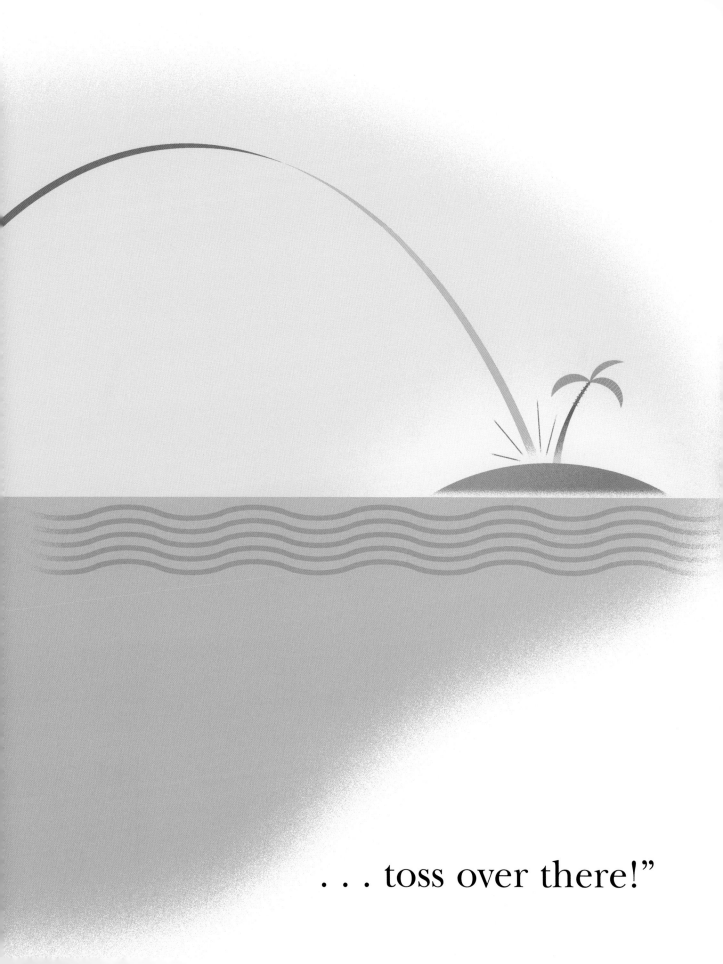

. . . toss over there!"

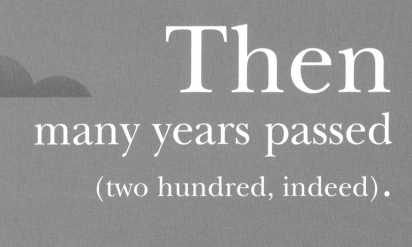

Then
many years passed
(two hundred, indeed).

That big lemon
orchard's now
nothing but
------------------weed.

Yet on that small island,
up sprouted a seed.

It started as one
and soon became many—

red lemon trees
in a grove of near twenty!

The islanders loved them,
those lemons of red.
They'd eat them in cupcakes
and bake them in bread.

And if yellow lemons
were always a treat,
the red lemon versions
were six times as sweet!

So now people travel
'cross oceans and seas
to eat the sweet fruit . . .

. . . from the red lemon trees.

For Ed Dyson

Visit us on the Web!
randomhouse.com/kids

Educators and librarians, for a variety of teaching tools, visit us at randomhouse.com/teachers

The Library of Congress has cataloged the hardcover edition of this work as follows:
Staake, Bob. The red lemon / by Bob Staake.—1st ed.
p. cm.
Summary: Farmer McPhee's yellow lemons are ready to be picked and made into lemonade, pies, and muffins, but when
a red lemon is found in the crop and discarded, it eventually yields some surprises.
ISBN 978-0-375-83593-3 (trade) — ISBN 978-0-375-93593-0 (lib. bdg.)
[1. Lemon—Fiction. 2. Stories in rhyme.] I. Title.
PZ8.3.S778Red 2006   [E]—dc22   2005009854

ISBN 978-0-307-97846-2 (pbk.)

MANUFACTURED IN CHINA   10 9 8 7 6
First Dragonfly Books Edition